Little Red Riding Hood

Retold by Rob Lloyd Jones
Illustrated by Lorena Alvarez

Once upon a time there was a little girl called Little Red Riding Hood.

She loved how her ruby red cloak swished and swayed as she skipped around her bedroom.

Little Red Riding Hood lived by a creaky old forest, where her mother kept bees...

...and her father chopped down trees.

One day, Little Red Riding Hood's
mother gave her a pot of honey.

"Will you take this to Grandma?"

Birds swooped
and chirped as
Little Red Riding Hood
skipped happily
through the trees.

"Hello, Little Red Riding
Hood," called her father.
But someone else was
watching her too...

A WOLF!

The wolf licked his lips and wagged his tail as he thought about eating Little Red Riding Hood for lunch.

He could have followed her and gobbled her up, but this was a cunning and crafty wolf, who loved to sneak around and set clever traps.

Snickering and snarling, the wolf laid a large net on the path between the trees.

His tail twitched as Little Red Riding Hood skipped closer and closer...

...and skipped right over the net.

Mumbling and muttering,
the wolf dug a deep hole,
and covered it with sticks
and leaves.

His eyes bulged, as
Little Red Riding Hood
skipped closer and closer...

...and skipped
right over the hole.

The wolf had one last plan. Grinning and giggling, he crept to Grandma's cottage, and knocked on the door.

Rap!

Rap!

He waited...

and waited...

...and then gobbled Grandma up in one hungry gulp. "Deeeelicious!" the wolf chortled. "Now for the main course."

The wolf's grin grew wider as he pulled on Grandma's clothes and leaped into her bed. "I'm so crafty!" he chuckled. "I'm the cleverest creature in the forest."

He waited... and waited...
    until Little Red Riding Hood skipped into the cottage.

"Hello Grandma," said Little Red Riding Hood.
"I've brought you some honey."

Little Red Riding Hood came closer.

"Oh Grandma, what **big** ears you have."

"All the better to **hear you** with, my dear," said the wolf.

"Oh Grandma, what **big** eyes you have."

"All the better to **see you** with, my dear."

"Oh Grandma, what **big** hairy hands you have."

"All the better to **hug you** with, my dear."

Little Red Riding Hood stepped back.
"Um... Grandma, what **big** teeth you have."

"All the better to **eat you** with!" snarled the wolf.

Hooting and howling, the greedy wolf burst from the bed and swallowed Little Red Riding Hood in one enormous gulp.

With a full tummy and
a happy smile, the wolf fell
into a deep and dreamy sleep.

He didn't see
Little Red Riding Hood's
father at the window.

With a mighty roar,
Little Red Riding Hood's
father stormed into
the cottage.

He chopped open the wolf's
tummy, and Little Red
Riding Hood and Grandma
came tumbling out.

Now, Grandma had a cunning and crafty plan too...

Little Red Riding Hood gathered stones from outside,
and dropped some into the wolf's tummy.

Then Grandma
stitched his
tummy up.

When the wolf woke,
he howled and howled and
howled again. Each time
he moved, the stones
rattled inside him.

"I'll never be able
to sneak around and set
cunning traps," he moaned,
as he fled back to the forest.

Now all the wolf could eat were worms and beetles and slow little bugs.

He was never cunning or crafty again.

Gotcha!

And Little Red Riding Hood skipped
all the way home.

About the story

Little Red Riding Hood was first written down around 200 years ago, by brothers Jacob and Wilhelm Grimm, who lived in Germany. They collected lots of other well-known tales, including *Sleeping Beauty* and *Snow White.*

Edited by Lesley Sims
Designed by Laura Nelson

First published in 2016 by Usborne Publishing Ltd., Usborne House, 83-85 Saffron Hill, London EC1N 8RT, England. www.usborne.com Copyright © 2016 Usborne Publishing Ltd.